# KODOMO
### CHILDREN OF JAPAN

SUSAN KUKLIN

# KODOMO

## CHILDREN OF JAPAN

子供

G. P. Putnam's Sons     New York

G. P. Putnam's Sons, a division of The Putnam & Grosset Group,
200 Madison Avenue, New York, NY 10016.
G. P. Putnam's Sons, Reg. U.S. Pat. & Tm. Off.
Published simultaneously in Canada. Printed in Singapore.
Book designed by Donna Mark and Songhee Kim.
Lettering by David Gatti. Text set in New Baskerville.
Japanese calligraphy on title page by Satomi Ichikawa.

Library of Congress Cataloging-in-Publication Data
Kuklin, Susan. Kodomo : children of Japan / Susan Kuklin. p.   cm.
1. Japan—Social life and customs—1945—Juvenile literature.
2. Children—Japan—Juvenile literature.   I. Title.
DS822.5.K82    1995   952.04′9′083—dc20   94-15417   CIP   AC
ISBN 0-399-22613-3
1   3   5   7   9   10   8   6   4   2
First Impression

This book is in celebration
of the differences and the similarities of
*kodomo* everywhere.

# ACKNOWLEDGMENTS

This book would not have been possible without the support and guidance of two organizations:

The Radiation Effects Research Foundation (RERF), Hiroshima and Japan National Tourist Organization (JNTO)

I would also like to voice my thanks and love to the following friends and colleagues:

In Hiroshima:
First and foremost, Dr. Seymour Abrahamson, Chief of Research at RERF. His encouragement, insights, and hospitality helped make this an extraordinary adventure.

The families, teachers and classmates of my pals, Eri Kodama, Nozomi Shinmoto, and Ai Enami.

Two very dear friends: my excellent translator, Morita Takako, and my *organisateur supérieur*, Akiko Enami.

In Kyoto:
The families and teachers of my partners, Keiko Konishi, Masaaki Hasegawa, Masako Nakata, and Natsuko Shiojiri.

The remarkable volunteer translators from Kyoto's JNTO: Yuko Asano, Miki Kodera, Hiroki Kato, and Yoko Okunishi.

In the U.S. and Tokyo:
Maria Y. Heffner and Hiroko Tani (New York), and Mihoko Suzuki (Tokyo) of JNTO.

My editor, Refna Wilkin, and designers, Donna Mark, Songhee Kim, and Cecilia Yung.

Keiko and Greg Kasza; and the best traveling partner ever, my husband, Bailey.

**B**ecause I have been an admirer of Asian art and literature throughout my adult life, I was delighted to have the opportunity to visit Japan in 1993. I met many warm and wonderful people. With their help I was able to write and photograph *Kodomo: Children of Japan*. *Kodomo* is the Japanese word for children.

While spending time with the participating families, I was repeatedly made aware that the Japanese see nature as a symbol of feelings and ideas. Birds, blossoms, and the seasons trigger emotional responses. Literature and poetry regularly include images from nature. Following this tradition, I have included representations of nature wherever possible to reflect the subject matter.

Although I shared many fascinating and enjoyable experiences with the families, teachers, and translators, it wasn't possible to include all of them in this book. For example, I was sorry not to cover *Haiku* poetry, flower arranging, and painting. I chose to describe the things that each child wanted readers from other countries to know about.

While working on *Kodomo,* I thought it would be interesting to include Japanese terms in the text in order to give readers a sense of this beautiful, difficult language. When a word is introduced, it is usually followed by a *kanji* character. Sometimes, however, it is necessary to use *hiragana, katakana,* or a combination of the two. These forms of writing are explained on page 46.

# PART ONE

# A Way of Life

## HIROSHIMA
### The City of Peace

At the beginning of March, *ume* 梅 (plum blossoms) peek out from their rugged boughs, marking the start of spring for *Nipponjin* 日本人, Japanese people. In Hiroshima, children eagerly prepare for the end of their school term and the beginning of vacation.

Eri, Nozomi, and Ai are three Japanese children who live in Hiroshima. Much of their lives is devoted to studying, but not all of it. There is enough time for running around and having fun.

**ERI, 8 years old**

*Most Sundays, when the family is together, Eri's mother makes a Japanese-style breakfast that might include* miso 味噌 *soup, pickled plum, a raw egg, dried seaweed, broiled fish, and green tea.*

Every morning at 7:30 sharp, my mother sits at the foot of my bed and gives my legs and shoulders a few shakes to wake me up for school. I get up and get dressed. Even though most public school students wear uniforms, we do not.

My mother is already dressed and has made breakfast for the other members of our family. My fourteen-year-old brother, Kazuhiro, is about to leave for school. My father, a doctor, has long gone to the institute where he works.

On school days, my mom makes a Western-style breakfast

10

of milk, cereal or eggs, bread, and a vegetable such as spinach, tomato, or cucumber.

After breakfast, I rush out to meet my big school sister. Fifth- and sixth-graders act as big sisters or brothers to us younger kids. One of their jobs is to make sure we get to school on time.

In the schoolyard, my classmates settle down for the morning ceremony called *chōrei* 朝礼. *Chōrei* brings everybody together before starting the day. An upper-school student makes announcements about school activities and leads us in a few songs. Even grownups in most businesses and large companies have *chōrei* before beginning the workday.

*In Japan, the academic year consists of three semesters: April to July, September to December, and January to March. Children attend school five days a week, with extra half-day classes on Saturday twice a month.*

Our teacher takes us upstairs to our classroom. Before entering the room, we take off our shoes, place them in the shoe rack, and put on slippers. It is customary to wear slippers inside houses, schools, temples, and even some restaurants. When I was little, I was taught never to bring the outside dirt inside. I think that's why we never wear shoes indoors.

Our language is complicated. We spend a lot of class time learning how to write it.

*Kanji* 漢字 is the hard stuff. Our teacher says, "Today we will learn the *kanji* for 'far.' " He writes the *kanji* with white chalk. "Remember that *kanji* you learned for the word garden? When you take the middle of 'garden' out of its box and add two strokes (lines) on the sides, the *kanji* becomes 'far.' "

We are also taught the correct stroke order. Our teacher uses different colored chalk to teach this. Order is very important because it helps us to have clear, beautiful writing.

After school is a very busy time for me. Monday I go to swimming class. Thursday I take piano lessons. Friday I have English conversation at the *juku* 塾 (after-school academic study institute). And Saturday afternoon I have calligraphy class. Today is Friday. At three o'clock, I go home and snack on cookies and milk. I have one and a half hours before the English *juku* starts. That gives me time to help

my mother with the marketing. I get to choose the fruits, vegetables, and flowers. While my mother goes off to buy the boring stuff, like milk and eggs, I stop off at the candy section. I use my allowance to buy candy and comic books.

Later at home, while my mother prepares dinner, I do my homework. I like to keep my desk neat because this is my own private spot. Next to school, I spend most time here.

*Japanese money is called yen* 円 *. About 100* yen *is equal to one U.S. dollar. A hundred* yen *can buy a candy bar.*

**NOZOMI, 9 years old**

I live in an apartment with my parents, my sisters, Miki (six) and Saki (five), and my brother, Kazuki (three). At home, we wear blue jeans or sweats, but at our public school we wear uniforms.

Our teacher encourages us to speak up and have fun while we learn. Sometimes I worry that visitors will think that our class is full of loudmouths because we make a lot of noise. Math, for example, is an especially loud subject.

"Ninety-five plus seven." The teacher calls out numbers fast. We quickly move beads back and forth to figure out the answers. In our school, we learn mathematics with a *soroban* 算盤 (abacus).

As soon as we know the answer, we raise our hands.

"Fifty-eight plus forty-six." All hands go up.

"Nozomi?" Our teacher calls on me.

"One hundred four."

"*Gomeisan* ごめいさん," shout all the other kids in really loud voices. ("Correct answer.") Whew!

After a while, we quiet down and our teacher writes a series of numbers on the board. We work out the answers silently at our desks. The kids who made mistakes during the calling out time go to the front of the room for additional practice with the teacher. When the lesson is over, we applaud our teacher.

*The* soroban, *which is used for counting and computing, is made of a frame holding parallel rods strung with movable beads.*

Lunchtime is everybody's favorite subject. Those students whose turn it is to be the servers put on white smocks and surgical masks before they fetch the food. Meanwhile, the rest of us rearrange the desks to make buffet and lunch tables. Once the servers return with large pots of food, everyone, including the teacher, puts on a mask as we line up for lunch. Our masks are a precaution against germs.

**AI, 14 years old**

On special occasions like New Year's Day, I dress up in my *kimono* 着物 . This is very important to me because the *kimono* belonged to my mother when she was my age. Now that it is mine, I know that I must take good care of it. My *kimono* is carefully folded and wrapped in rice paper.

There are several steps to getting dressed. Over my underwear, I wear a *juban* じゅばん, a silk robe that is a little shorter than the *kimono*. I use a red silk sash to hold it together. Once the *juban* is carefully tied, it is time to put on the *kimono*.

*In olden times, a Japanese woman often dressed in a long robe called a* kimono. *Men wore* kimono, *too, but they were not as elaborate. Nowadays Japanese people generally wear Western clothing, but the* kimono *is still popular as formal dress.*

19

My mother folds the sides of the *kimono* left over right. If she folded it in reverse, it would mean bad luck because that is the way the *kimono* is folded on a dead person.

When my mother wraps the *kimono* around me, she lets the *juban* show through at the neck. Then comes a long green embroidered silk sash called an *obi* 帯 that holds the *kimono* together. There are many ways to tie the *obi*. This one is called the *fukura suzume* ふくら雀, butterfly bow, and it's my favorite.

The outfit is finished off with a pink silk cord to keep the *obi* and *kimono* tightly closed and a third, softer sash to fill in the space between the top of the *obi* and the *kimono*.

The display of dolls in Ai's home is in honor of Hina-Matsuri 雛祭り (Girls' Day). On this day, families with daughters celebrate to assure their daughters' future happiness. Hina-Ningyo 雛人形 (miniature dolls), which are replicas of the ancient Heian royal court in Kyoto, are placed on a large stand covered with bright red cloth. The emperor and empress are on the highest level. Each level down represents members of their court. Peach blossoms, symbolizing a happy marriage, decorate the sides.

Hina-Ningyo dolls are displayed during the girls' festival. Warrior dolls, which are replicas of the knights known as samurai 侍, are displayed during the boys' festival. These are not every-day toys to be played with. They are ceremonial dolls that are often handed down from generation to generation. Like Ai's kimono, this collection belonged to her mother when she was a child.

21

## ABOUT HIROSHIMA

Hiroshima is important in world history. At the end of World War II, the United States dropped the first atomic bomb there, on August 6, 1945, at 8:15 A.M. The city was completely flattened and more than 100,000 people died immediately. As years passed, many people died from the radiation effects of the atomic bomb.

Two years after the atom bomb was dropped, the citizens of Hiroshima held a peace ceremony. Their theme was "No more Hiroshimas." The epicenter, or exact spot where the bomb exploded, was turned into a park called *Heiwa Kinen*

*Kōen* 平和記念公園 (Peace Memorial Park). People go there to pray for peace. In the center of the park is a flame that burns continuously. It will be extinguished only when there are no more atomic weapons.

Near the burning flame, there is a memorial to a young girl called Sadako. Sadako was only two years old when the atomic bomb was dropped on Hiroshima. As a result of the radiation from it, she developed leukemia when she was twelve. At one point, a friend visited her in the hospital and reminded her of the fable about the crane that lived a healthy life for a thousand years. Sadako began to fold paper *origami* 折り紙 cranes as an offering to the gods in return for good health. She managed to fold six hundred and forty-four cranes before she died.

Sadako's memorial is considered a symbol of peace and disarmament. Children like Eri, Nozomi, and Ai, along with people from all over the world, visit it. In her honor, they leave thousands of paper cranes with wishes for peace.

# PART TWO

# TRADITIONAL ACTIVITIES

## KYOTO
### The Ancient Capital of Japan

In April, the *sakura* 桜 (cherry blossoms) burst into bouquets of color. The cherry tree affects the *Nipponjin* in an emotional way. Ancient myths tell how the petals fall while they are still at the height of their beauty. The *samurai* regarded the blossoms' characteristics as symbols of grace and also of the certainty of death. Today the Japanese consider the *sakura* the flower that best symbolizes their country. One of the most beautiful places to view them in full bloom is in Kyoto.

Keiko, Masaaki, Masako, and Natsuko live in Kyoto, and like many children, they participate in activities from ancient times, along with modern ones.

**KEIKO, 9 years old**

Kendō, *the art of fencing, is a traditional martial art whose origins go back to the seventh or eighth century. In the sixteenth century, the* samurai *refined it to include ethical qualities such as courage, honesty, and patience. Today* kendō *is considered both a modern sport and a fun way to absorb the teachings of the noble* samurai.

When my brother started taking *kendō* 剣道 classes, my mother took me with her to watch him. It looked cool. As soon as I was old enough, I decided to try it, too. Every Saturday morning, I become a *samurai*.

Before entering the *dōjō* 道場 (exercise hall), I take off my shoes and place them against the wall. Barefoot, I enter and bow to greet the other *kenshi* 剣士 (people who practice *kendō*). In the dressing room, I change into my *hakama* 袴 (skirt-like trousers), red *dō* 胴 (chest protector), *tare* 垂れ (hip protector), and *keikogi* 稽古着 (jacket).

At the command of *sensei* 先生 (teacher), we stand up, bow, and enter the fencing area. We place our *shinai* 竹刀 (swords) in a huge star formation at the center of the hall. Then we run around the star as fast as we can. The floor of the *dōjō* feels cold, but this exercise helps to warm us up. After a few minutes of stretching, we are ready for action.

*Sensei* reviews the strokes that we have already learned. He tells us to empty our minds. "Forget about your friends, your homework, even forget the cherry blossoms outside the *dōjō*. Only after emptying your minds will you be able to use speed, strength, and form to beat your opponent." I close my eyes and think of nothing.

*Sensei* stands in the center of the *dōjō* and raises his *shinai*. We all line up, race forward, and strike it. So far, I have learned three kinds of strokes with my *shinai*. The *men-uchi* 面打ち (stroke to the head), the *kote-uchi* 小手打ち (stroke to the arm), and the *dō-uchi* 胴打ち (stroke to the body). If we do not use the correct form, we must go back and do it again.

Once we've all taken our turns, we finish dressing at our places at one end of the fencing area. My father, who also takes *kendō*, told me that the dressing ritual has gone on for hundreds of years. We sit with our legs tucked under our bodies. My *shinai* is by my right side. The rest of my equipment is placed in front of me.

Around the top of my head I wrap a *hachimaki* 鉢巻き (towel-like cloth that is used to keep the sweat from dripping down into the eyes). This also acts as a cushion for the *men* 面 (face mask). The last item is the *kote* 小手 (gloves). Now I am a true *samurai*, ready for battle. I like dressing up in *kendō* armor. I look cool.

I face my opponent. At the beginning and end of each fight, we bow to each other. As we battle, our *shinai* swish through the air. I'm glad I am wearing my *men* to protect my face. But it gets in the way when I want to tell my friend a secret.

At the end of the lesson, we take our original places at the back of the *dōjō* and remove our *men* and *hachimaki.* Facing *sensei,* we meditate for a while. This helps to cool us down. Then we listen to his comments.

After *kendō* class, my mother and I return to our family's restaurant in Fushimi, a suburb of Kyoto. While my parents prepare *sushi* 寿司 for lunch, my grandfather and I take a walk. My grandfather is the third oldest man in our neighborhood, and everyone is very respectful when they greet him. On our walk, we see a beautiful *jinja* 神社 (*Shintō* shrine) with many cherry trees in bloom. We go in and say a prayer together. Walks with my grandfather are even more special to me than my *kendō* suit.

**MASAAKI, 8 years old**

Three evenings a week, Father and I take *jūdō* 柔道 classes at the *dōjō*. My father is an expert—a *kuro obi* 黒帯 (black belt). Our teacher, Ryozo Yamazaki, is a famous *jūdō sensei* who has trained many athletes, including his daughter.

In the beginning, I was just learning to fall. I asked *sensei* if I could be in a match. He said, "Keep practicing falling. In order to learn to fight, you must be patient."

So I am learning to be patient and to concentrate. My father says that is the *jūdō* spirit.

After our warm-up exercises, we do tumbling. *Sensei* says,

"Make your mind like a blank piece of paper." I concentrate real hard. "Two sides of the paper need to be filled, the physical side and the spiritual side. You cannot have one without the other. Only then will you be able to do a good tumble."

Then one student hunkers down in the middle of the mat. One by one we run toward him, jump over him, make a circle with our body, and land on the mat. The landing must have one loud sound. WAMP! That's one way we know if we have fallen correctly.

After everyone takes a turn, *sensei* adds another student to the center of the floor. Then another. And another, until four students are hunkered down. The rest of us tumble over them.

*Jūdō is another traditional martial art. The first school was founded by Jigoro Kano in 1882. The aim of jūdō is not just to win contests, but to train the mind as well as the body. Its name comes from the saying jū yoku go o seisu ("softness overcomes hardness.") The jū of jūdō means "gentle" or "soft."*

Afterward we get the chance to practice our throws by working one-to-one. Before and after each throw, we bow to each other. A *kuro obi* watches over each set of *jūdōka* 柔道家 (person who practices *jūdō*). They instruct us and make sure that we do the throws properly. They also watch out for our safety. Sometimes my father becomes my instructor. That's neat.

I lift a big kid over my shoulders and throw him down on the mat. I feel really good when I throw my opponent. I feel strong. "It's payback time," shouts my opponent. "I'm going to do the throw next time." Uh-oh.

After the last throws, we do push-ups and sit-ups to build muscle. At the end of practice, we take our places at the edge of the mat, facing *sensei*. With our legs tucked under us, we close our eyes and meditate for about five minutes. This gives us a chance to clear our heads and cool down. At the sound of *sensei's* voice, we open our eyes and listen to his lecture.

*Sensei* reminds us of an old saying in Japan. " 'A big tree is stiff and can break. But bamboo is flexible and bends.' *Jūdō* is like bamboo. *Jūdō* teaches people to be strong, but flexible so that they bend but do not break."

**MASAKO, 12 years old**

Shodō, *also known as calligraphy, is a traditional art form that is very popular in Japan. In ancient times, excellent writing was believed to be an indication of a person with superior inner character.* Shodō *varies according to the beauty of the strokes, the color of the ink, what is being expressed, and the personality of the writer.*

Once a week, I go to the center to study *shodō* 書道 . At the long, low drawing tables, I sit on a floor cushion and prepare my materials. The paper is made from rice stalks and is very delicate. I use a *futofude* 太筆 (thick brush) for the assigned characters and a *hosofude* 細筆 (thin brush) to draw my name and smaller characters. *Sumi* 墨 (Chinese ink) comes in a stick that must be made into a liquid. Making your own *sumi* is an important part of *shodō*. For about fifteen minutes, I rub the ink stick on a rectangular *suzuri* 硯 (ink stone) that has a small pool of water at one

☛ Hiroi 広い *means "wide," oo* 大 *means "big," and zora* 空 *means "sky."*

end. I rub the *sumi* in a circular motion, from the pool of water to the base of the *suzuri*. This process gives me time to slow down and relax. If I mix the ink too thick or too thin, the characters that I draw will not be beautiful. My *sensei* can always tell if I've mixed the ink too quickly.

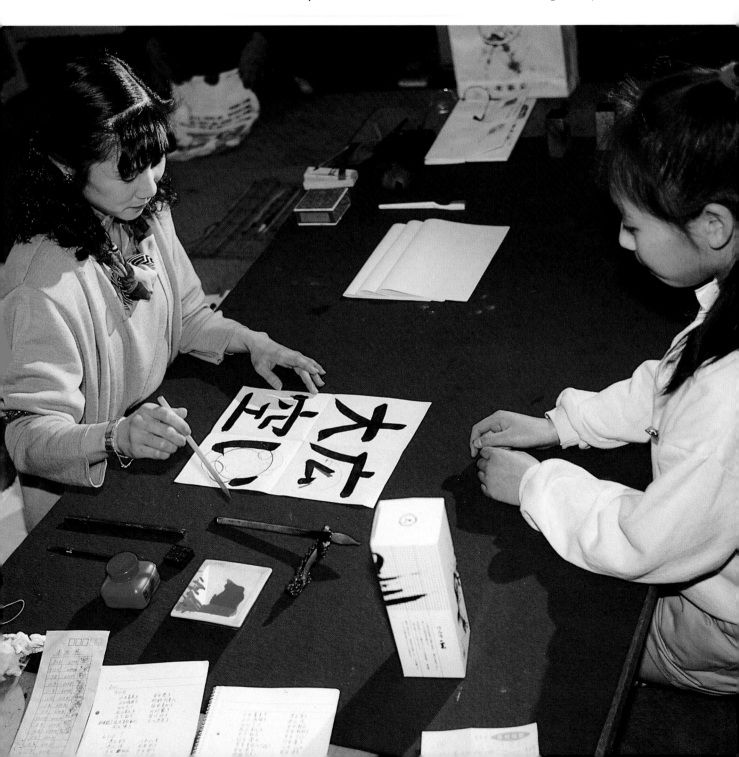

I learn by copying the works of a master calligrapher. Today's characters are *hiroi oozora* 広い大空. I close my eyes and fill my heart with the image of a beautiful, clear blue sky. It makes me feel light and happy.

As I draw, I sit very straight. I put one hand on my paper and hold my *futofude* straight up with the other. I must be very calm. I can't look around. I think only about the shape of the letter and the feeling of the sky. If I were to think about anything else, I would make mistakes. Even heavy breathing can show up in the stroke. My teacher says that the most important thing about *shodō* is to learn to concentrate.

I write my name and grade with my *hosofude.* After I write the day's characters a few times, I bring the best example to my *sensei.* If it is good, she circles the character in red. If it is not so good, she corrects it and I try again.

In my country, *shodō* is considered as important as poetry and painting. My sister, my mother, and my grandmother all study it. In fact, my parents have hung my *sensei's shodō* in a place of honor, the entrance hall of our house.

*Symbols of nature are often used to express emotional feelings. "Wide, big sky" (a standard beginner's phrase that contains basic strokes) conveys how the person should feel while doing shodō—light, airy, open.*

**NATSUKO, 9 years old**

My house is Western-style. My grandparents, however, live nearby in a traditional home. One of my chores is to rake their garden. I don't rake leaves. I rake pebbles. My grandfather taught me that when the ancient Japanese people migrated inland from the sea, they wanted to keep their memories of the ocean. Often pebbles or sand symbolize the ocean, rocks and bushes portray islands, and trees illustrate mountains or waterfalls. I like making furrows in the gravel to create the effect of rippling water.

Inside, my mother teaches me *sadō* 茶道 , the tradition of the tea ceremony. My mother says that *sadō* started long ago in China.

In my grandparents' *zashiki* 座敷 (formal room), my mother and I sit on the *tatami* 畳み (mat) in front of the tea set. Because the *tatami* is delicate, no one walks on it in slippers, only socks, stockings, or bare feet.

My mother helps me take out just the right amount of powdered green tea from a lacquered container. With a long wooden spoon, I drop the tea powder into a ceramic bowl. Very carefully, very slowly, I pour boiling water into the bowl. We are quiet, serious. All we hear is the bubbling water and the sound of the wooden whisk I use to stir the tea. After the tea becomes foamy, I turn the bowl so that the decorative design is facing the person who will drink it. With one hand I present the foamy tea to my mother, and she accepts it with two hands. Before my mother takes a sip, she turns the bowl clockwise one quarter around. This is called "declining to drink from the front of the bowl" and is a gesture of respect and humility. This makes me feel calm.

*Like the rock garden, sadō came from a school of the Buddhist religion called* Zenshū 禅宗 . Zenshū *emphasizes the importance of simple, beautiful surroundings.*

*For hundreds of years, women have been studying* sadō *before they marry as a way of acquiring grace and good manners.*

*In the eighteenth century, there were four famous choreographers: Fujima, Hanayagi, Wakayagi, and Nishikawa. Senzo Nishikawa started the Nishikawa ryū 流 (school) at that time. Today there are more than four hundred schools of dance in Japan. Nishikawa is one of the more popular forms.*

I am learning many traditions from my family and my many *sensei*. For example, I love Japanese dance. I am learning to dance in a style called *Nishikawa* 西川. Someday I hope to become a professional dancer, just like my *sensei*.

I started learning to dance on July 6, when I was six years old. One of our proverbs says that if you start something on that day, you will be good at it. At first I danced with other students, just like ballet class. After a while, our skills became different so we took individual lessons.

Professional dancers who perform in the Nishikawa style are considered members of the Nishikawa family and adopt their last name. For example, my *sensei* is called Mitsu Nishikawa. If I become good enough to become a professional, I will change my name to Natsuko Nishikawa.

At the dance studio, I change into a cotton robe called a *yukata* 浴衣 . Sometimes I dance beside my *sensei,* and other times she watches me and makes corrections. During the lesson, we hold umbrellas or fans. My *sensei* says that both the umbrella and the fan act as extensions of our arms. Rolling the umbrella is my absolute favorite part of the dance. When we dance, we are supposed to keep our faces very relaxed and kind of serious. But when I get behind my red umbrella, it is hard not to giggle.

*When performing Nishikawa, the dancer's feet never leave the floor. In Western ballet, the feet are turned out. In this form of Japanese dance, the feet are turned in. Every move, from the tilt of the head to the turn of the toe, is very slow and highly stylized.*

## ABOUT KYOTO

In 794 A.D., Emperor Kammu founded *Heian-kyō* 平安京, the capital of peace and tranquility. Life for the royal family and the court revolved around rituals. Many laws governed such daily activities as when members of the court could wash, cut their nails, travel, and even leave their house. Nonetheless, the *Heian Jidai* 平安時代 (Heian period) evolved into one of the most elegant and cultured in the history of civilization. Paintings, sculptures, and poetry portrayed compassion and serenity. About the year 1000, women began writing about court life in diaries and novels.

Lady Murasaki, a lady-in-waiting to the Empress, wrote the first known novel, *Genji Monogatari* (*The Tale of Genji*, 源氏物語), a story mainly about the amorous adventures of a prince called Genji.

Most of the beautiful temples and palaces in Kyoto were destroyed in the civil wars of the fifteenth and sixteenth centuries. But when Hideyoshi Toyotomi became regent at the end of the sixteenth century, he reunified the country and rebuilt Kyoto.

Today religion, history, and tradition are an integral part of daily life. There are countless festivals held throughout the year in and around the fifteen hundred or so *jinja* 神社 and *tera* 寺 (Buddhist temples). For example, when the cherry blossoms first appear, friends and families celebrate with picnics. Some people dress up in the ancient costumes of the Heian court and parade through the neighborhood.

For more than twelve hundred years, children like Keiko, Masaaki, Masako, and Natsuko have participated in the rich traditions of their fascinating country, *Nippon.*

Japanese isn't usually written in an alphabet. Each word normally has its own special mark, or ideogram. An ideogram is a character or symbol representing an idea or an object. Children must learn three forms of writing Japanese. They are *hiragana* ひらがな, *katakana* カタカナ, and *kanji* 漢字. These symbols can be used separately or they can be combined. Students start by learning *hiragana*.

*Hiragana* has rounded shapes. *Katakana* has angular shapes. Each has forty-six characters, with each character representing a syllable. Together they are known as the *kana* system. *Katakana* is used mainly for transcribing foreign names and words like "Harry," "pizza," and "baseball." Books for children and compositions by young students are generally written in *hiragana* with some *katakana* included.

*Kanji* characters were developed from ideograms brought to Japan from China. The complicated *kanji* are used generally to write nouns and to express poetic language. Each *kanji* ideogram represents an entire word, and must be memorized separately. By the end of this year, Eri will have learned four hundred ideograms in *kanji*.

Many *kanji* characters come from other characters. They build on each other. When strokes are added or subtracted, the meaning changes.

Japanese is usually written from top to bottom and from the right side of the page to the left. Books open from the reverse side of Western books.

# GLOSSARY

| | |
|---|---|
| *Chōrei* | Morning meeting |
| *Dō* | Chest protector worn during *kendō* |
| *Dō-uchi* | *Kendō* strike to the body |
| *Dōjō* | Exercise hall |
| *Fukura suzume* | Butterfly bow used to tie an *obi* |
| *Futofude* | Thick brush used in *shodō* (calligraphy) |
| *Genji Monogatari* | *The Tales of Genji,* the first known novel, which took place during the *Heian Jidai* |
| *Gomeisan* | Correct answer |
| *Hachimaki* | Towel used as a headband |
| *Hakama* | Skirt-like trousers worn during *kendō* |
| *Heian Jidai* | (794–1195 A.D.) A period in Japanese history when art, literature, and culture reached extraordinary sophistication. The Emperor founded his court in Kyoto. |
| *Heian-kyō* | Kyoto during the Heian period |
| *Heiwa Kinen Kōen* | Peace Memorial Park in Hiroshima |
| *Hina-Matsuri* | Girls' Day |
| *Hina-Ningyo* | Beautiful dolls that are replicas of an ancient Japanese court in Kyoto |
| *Hiragana* | A Japanese form of writing that is part of the *kana* system. It has forty-six symbols that represent syllables and can spell out various *kanji.* |
| *"Hiroi oozora"* | "Wide, big sky" |
| *Hosofude* | Thin brush used in *shodō* |
| *Jinja* | Shrine. A *Shintō* place of worship |
| *Juban* | A garment worn under the *kimono* |
| *Jūdō* | Hand-to-hand combat, or the way of the gentle path |
| *Jūdōka* | A person who practices *judō* |
| *Juku* | A private school held after public school classes where students continue to study academic subjects |
| *"Jū yoku go o seisu"* | "Softness overcomes hardness" |
| *Kana* | Combination of the *katakana* and *hiragana* forms of writing |
| *Kanji* | Chinese ideograms that are now part of the Japanese writing system. There are said to be about fifty thousand characters. Three thousand are commonly known, including the 1,945 "daily use" characters. |
| *Katakana* | A Japanese form of writing that is part of the *kana* system. It has forty-six symbols that represent syllables and is used to write foreign names and words such as "Harry," "baseball," "pizza," "television." |
| *Keikogi* | Jacket worn during *kendō* |
| *Kendō* | The art of fencing |

| | |
|---|---|
| *Kenshi* | A person who practices *kendō* |
| *Kimono* | Clothing, traditional Japanese robe |
| *Kodomo* | Children |
| *Kote* | Gloves or hand and forearm protector worn during *kendō* |
| *Kote-uchi* | *Kendō* strike to the arm |
| *Kuro Obi* | Black belt, the highest level of *judō* |
| *Lady Murasaki* | The first great novelist, who lived in the late eleventh century |
| *Men* | Face mask used in *kendō* |
| *Men-uchi* | *Kendō* strike to the head |
| *Miso* | Fermented soybean paste that is used in making soup or in a marinade for vegetables and fish |
| *Nippon* | Japan |
| *Nipponjin* | A Japanese person |
| *Nishikawa* | A school of Japanese classical dance |
| *Obi* | A sash worn with a *kimono* or a *yukata* |
| *Origami* | The art of paper folding |
| *Ryu* | School |
| *Sadō* | Traditional tea ceremony |
| *Sakura* | Cherry blossom |
| *Samurai* | Traditional knight |
| *Sensei* | Teacher |
| *Shinai* | Fencing sword used in *kendō* |
| *Shintō* | A traditional religion of Japan, marked by the worship of nature, spirits, and ancestors |
| *Shodō* | Calligraphy, or the art of fine writing |
| *Soroban* | An abacus. A manual counting and computing device consisting of a frame holding parallel rods strung with movable beads |
| *Sumi* | Black ink, made of soot from burned wood or oil mixed with fish bone, that is dried into a stick |
| *Sushi* | Vinegared rice topped or filled with raw fish, vegetables, or omelet |
| *Suzuri* | Inkstone used when doing *shodō* |
| *Tare* | Hip protector worn during *kendō* |
| *Tatami* | Thick mat made of rice straw |
| *Tera* | Temple, Buddhist place of worship |
| *Ume* | Plum blossom |
| *Yen* | Japanese money |
| *Yukata* | Clothing, a cotton robe |
| *Zashiki* | The most formal room in the house, used for entertaining |
| *Zenshū* | Zen Buddhism, a school of Buddhism that maintains that enlightenment can be attained through meditation, self-contemplation, and instinct rather than through studying scriptures |